You make me very HOPPY!

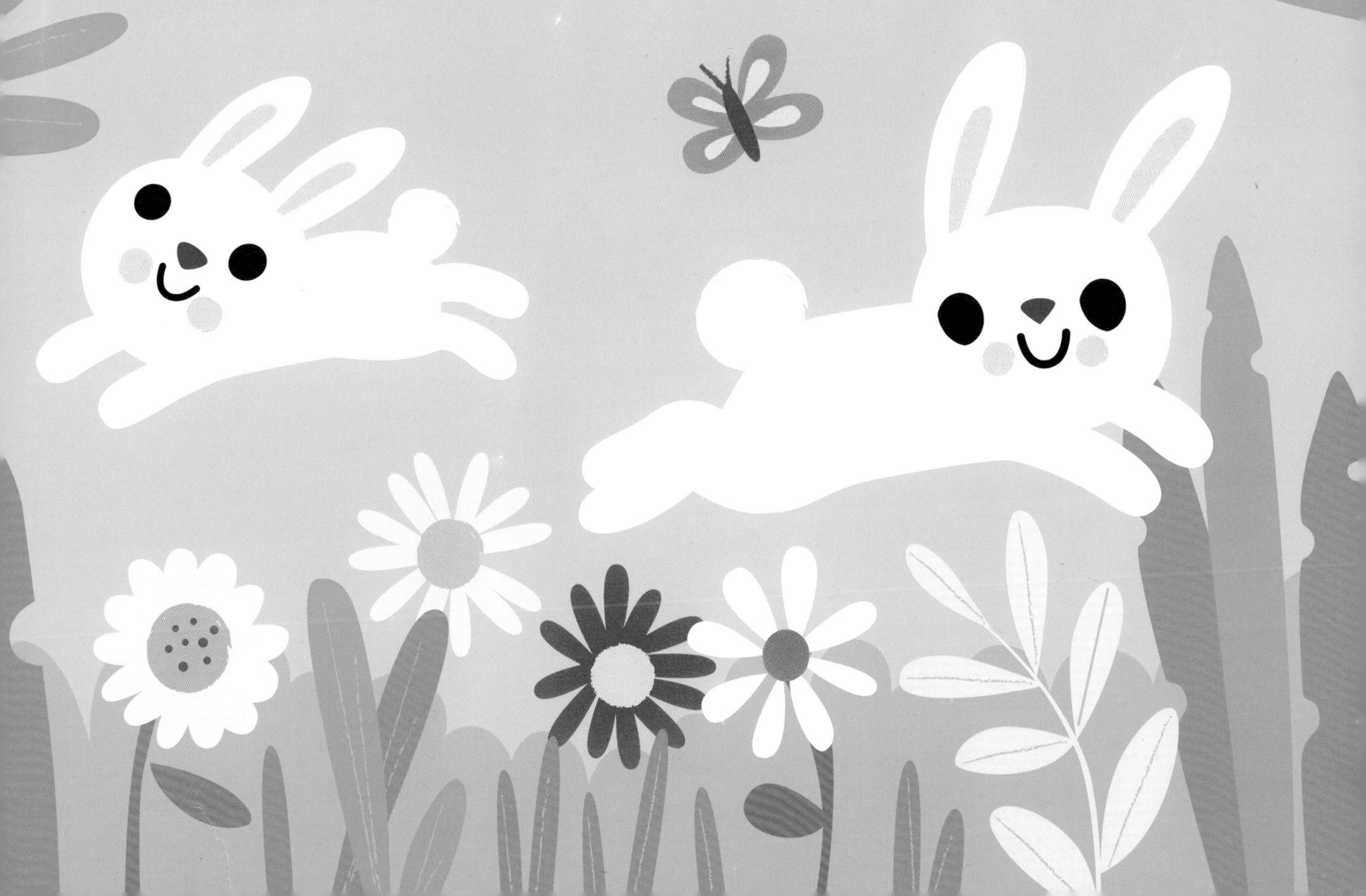

I

BULLIEVE

in you!

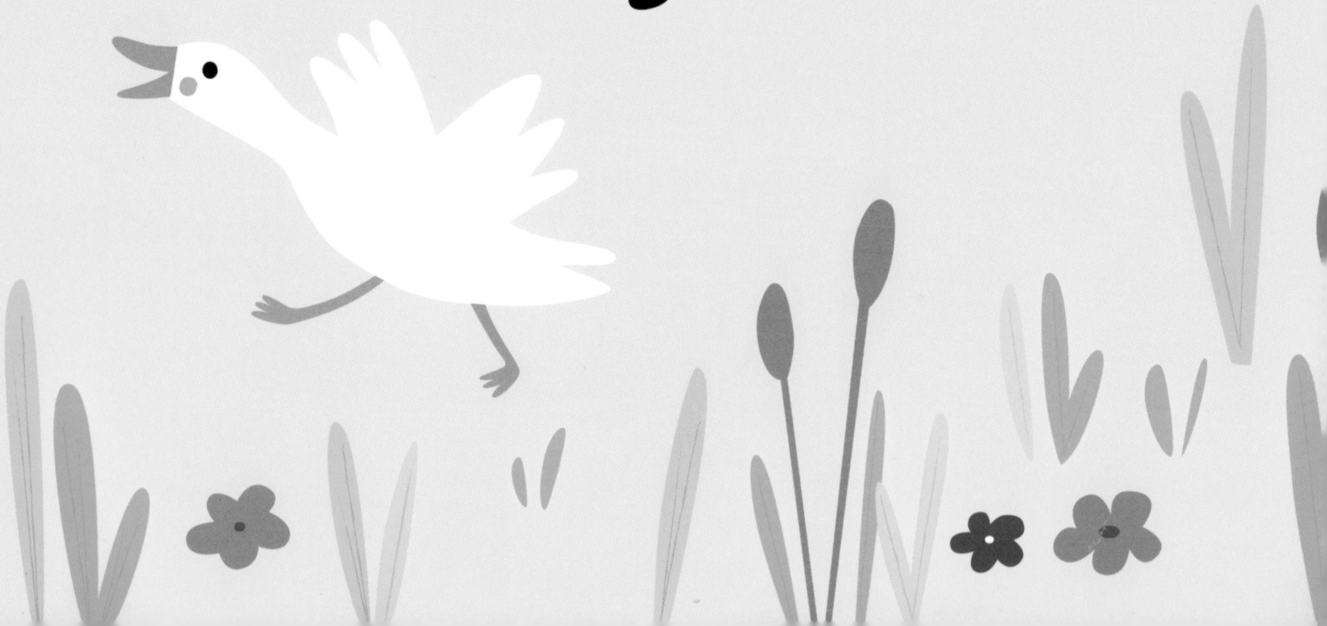

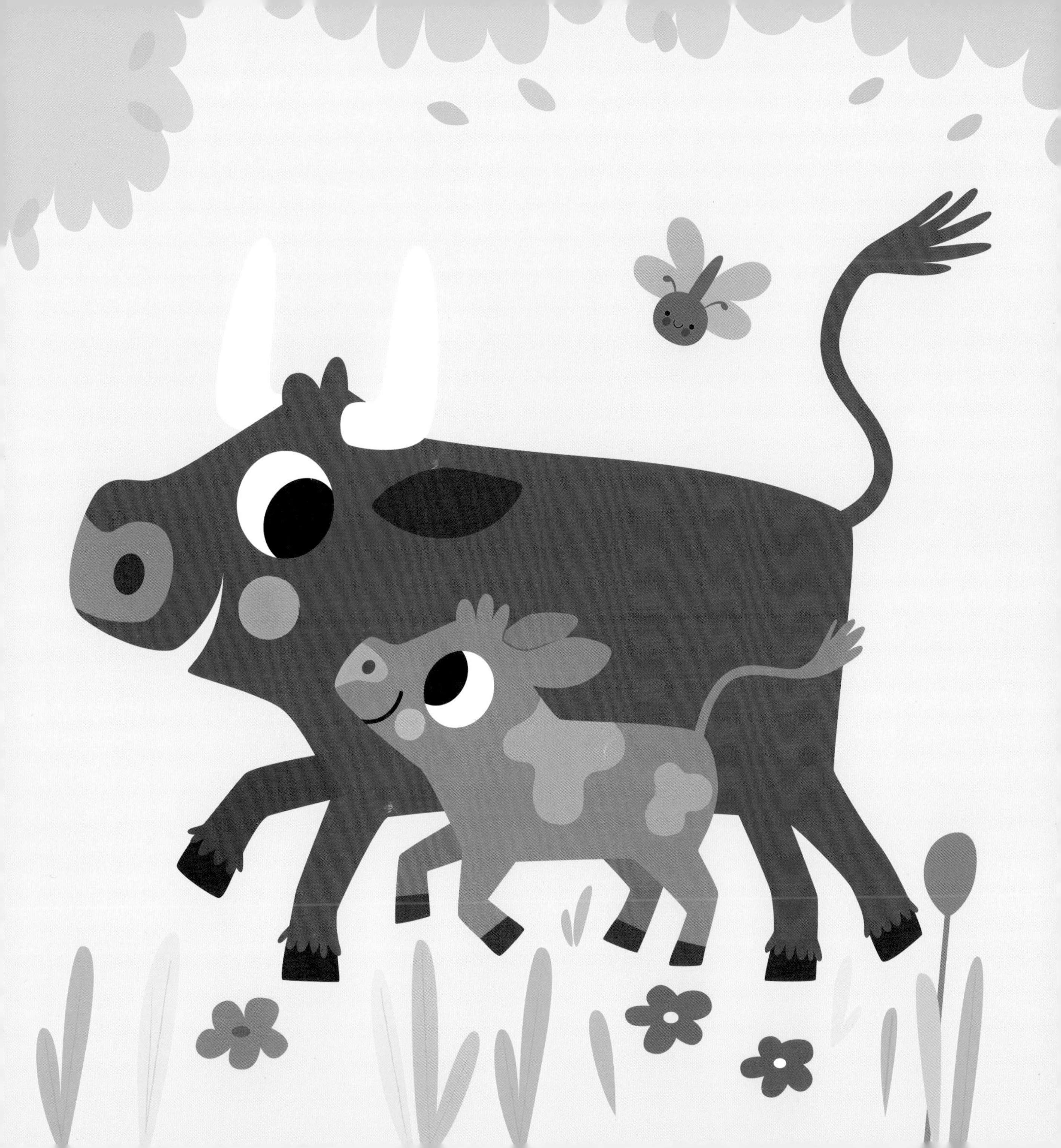

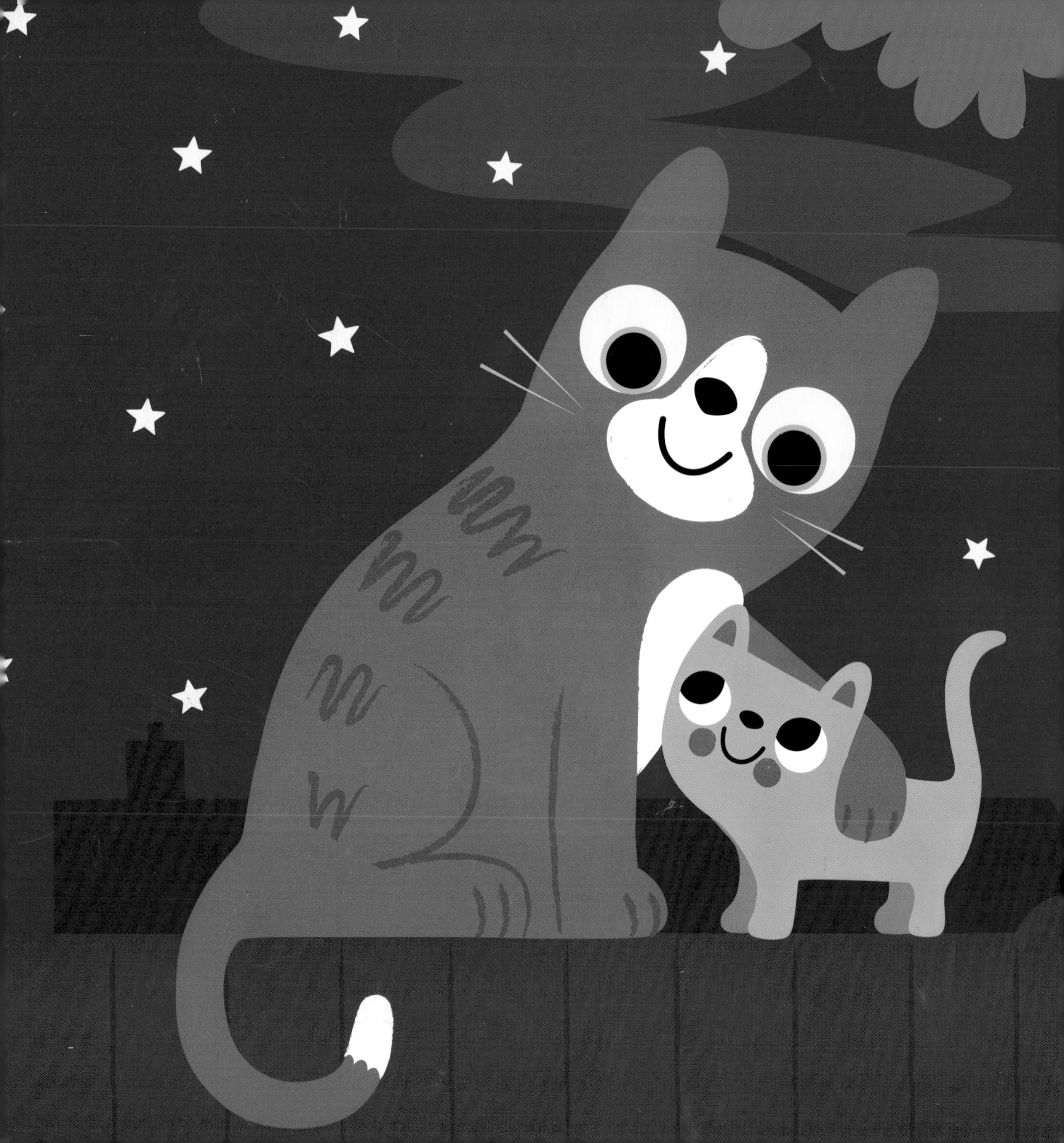

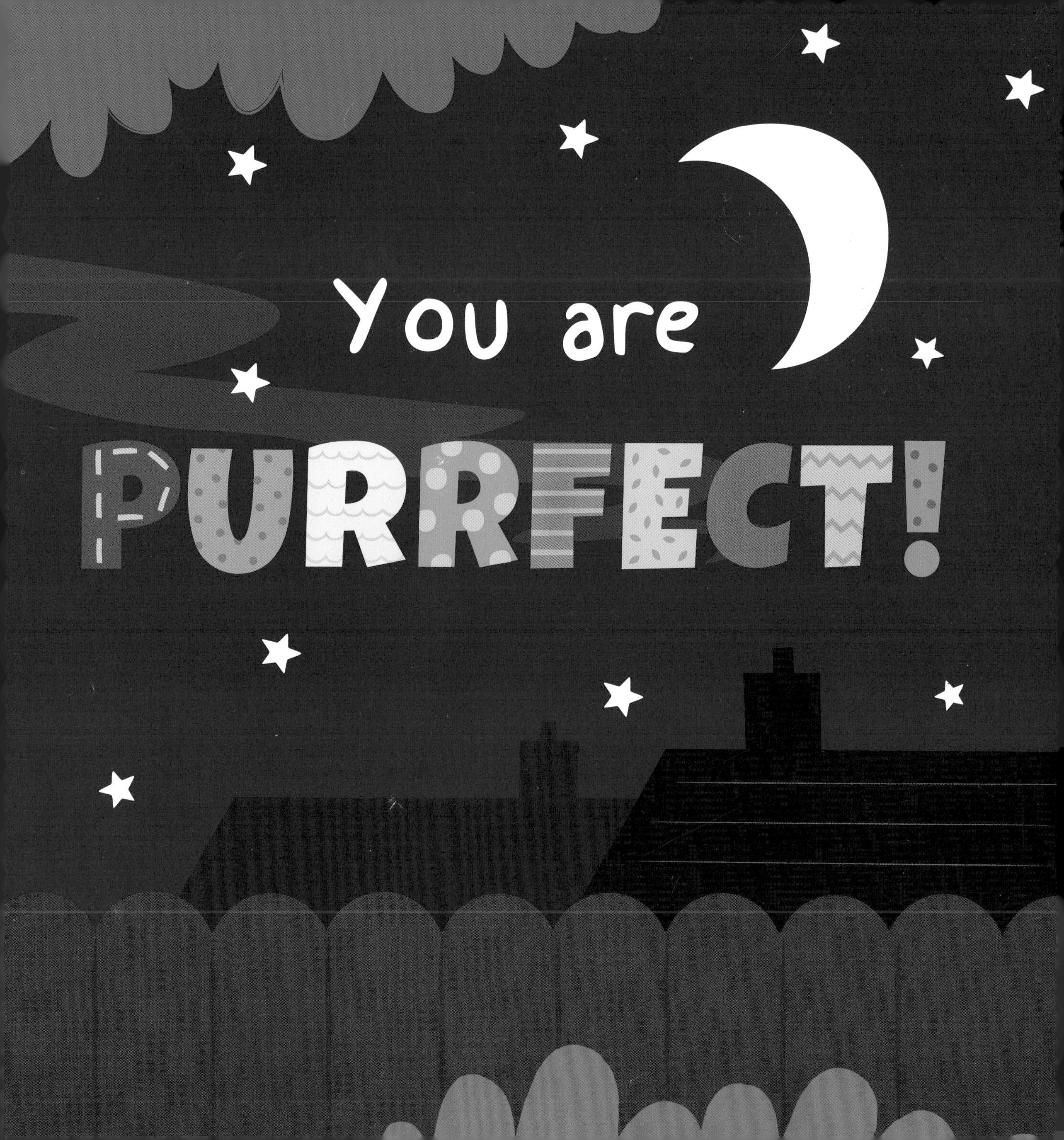

You are

PURRFECT!

Always

BEE

yourself!

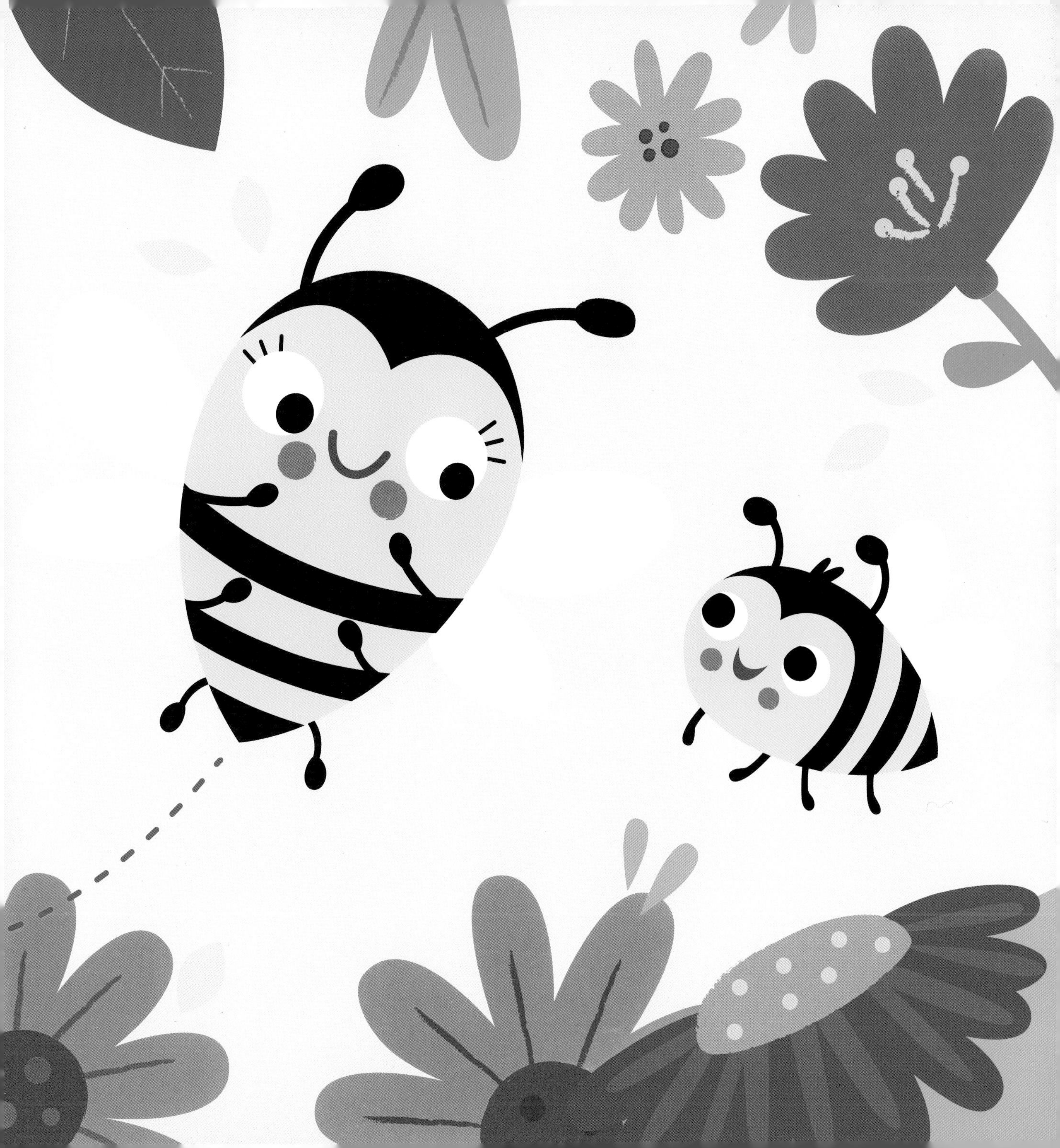

You're

ELEPHANT-TASTIC!

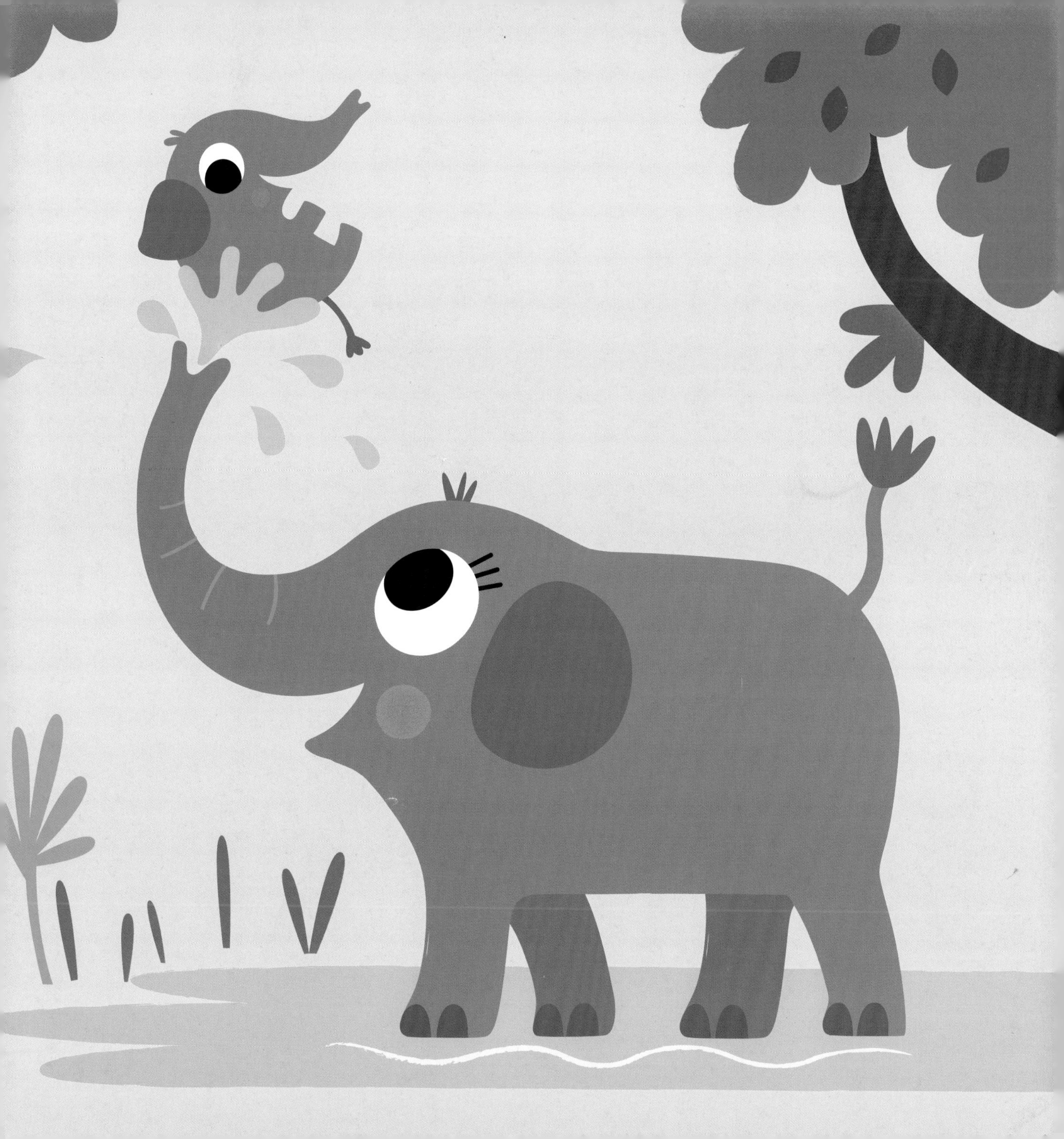

You're my best friend...

and i'm not

LION!

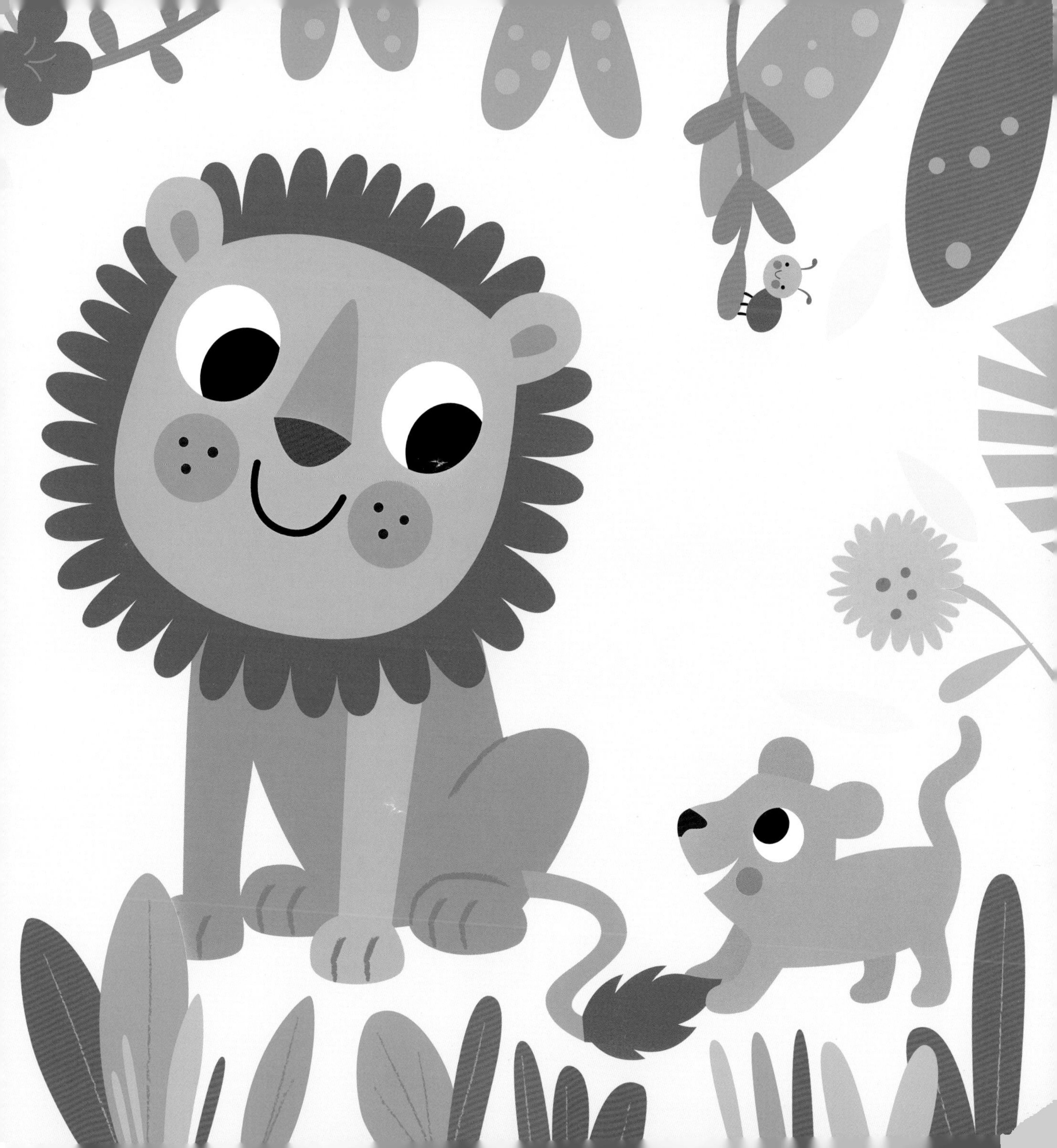

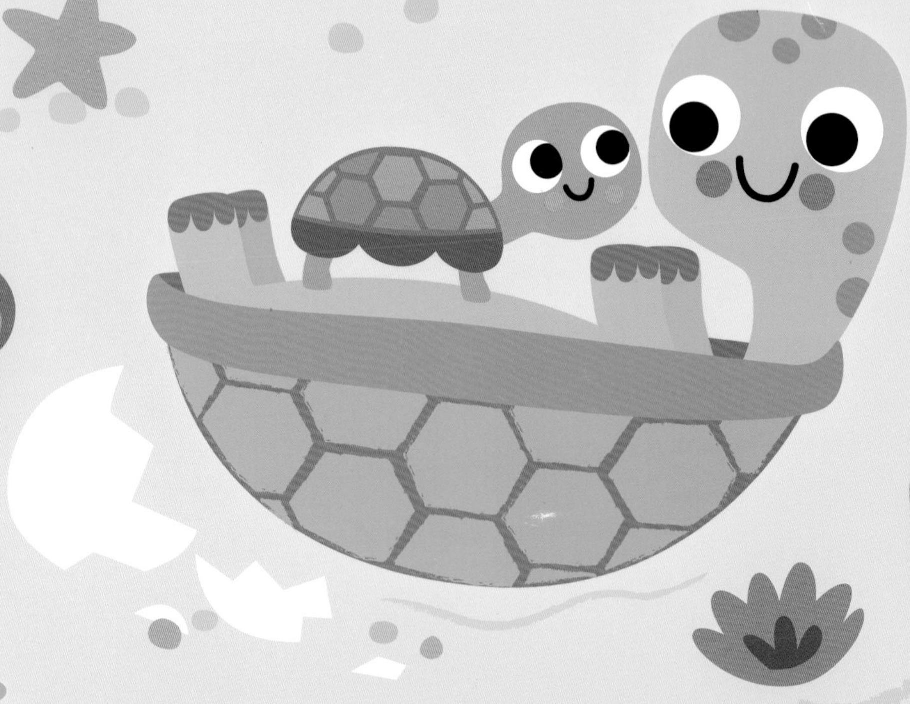

You're

TURTLEY

cute!